TATTOOS, TACOS, AND TIME

Tattoos, Tacos, and Time

A POETRY COLLECTION BY

ANGELA LEIGH

REDHAWK
PUBLICATIONS

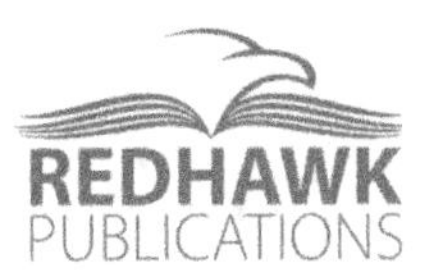

Tattoos, Tacos, and Time

ISBN: 979-8-89933-024-7 (Paperback)
Library of Congress Control Number: 2026910191

Cover, Book Design, and Illustration: Amber Zezeck

Printed in the United States of America.
First printing 2026.

Redhawk Publications
The Catawba Valley Community College Press
2550 Hwy 70 SE
Hickory, NC 28602
https://redhawkpublications.com

Dedicated to
every lover of love, every hopeless romantic, every heart that has felt love, lost love, and found love again. And to every heart still searching.

Author's Note

I used to think I hated poetry. What I came to realize is that I hated not understanding poetry. I dreaded being asked to explain what a poem meant, what I thought the poet intended to say. Of course, this was before I knew that poetry is simply another way of telling a story, one that has as much to say in what isn't written on the page as in what is. It was before I understood that poetry is art, and there is as much in the meaning the reader gleans as in what the author meant when they wrote the words. It's what I've come to love about poetry; that every time a poem is read, it means something new, something more, layers added with each reader's experience, with what each reader needs.

I've been writing poetry for a little over a decade. I've been writing poetry with intention for slightly less than that. The wider variety of poetry I read, the more I learned about the ways to express myself through poetry. Teaching poetry to ninth graders challenged me to expand my own writing, to explore styles of poetry I hadn't tried previously. With that in mind, you'll find free verse poetry in this collection, of course, as well as acrostic poems and haiku, both more challenging and complex styles of poetry than one might think on initial inspection. There's even a poem created around a series of text messages. One of my favorite things about poetry is the way you can "break the rules" of writing to convey your meaning. You'll find poems here inspired by my life - experiences, feelings, hopes, fears - as well as verse written in response to prompts, some slightly easier to consider than others.

Baring one's soul through poetry is such a vulnerable affair. Thank you for holding these delicate offerings with care as you read. I hope you find one that connects with you in some positive way.

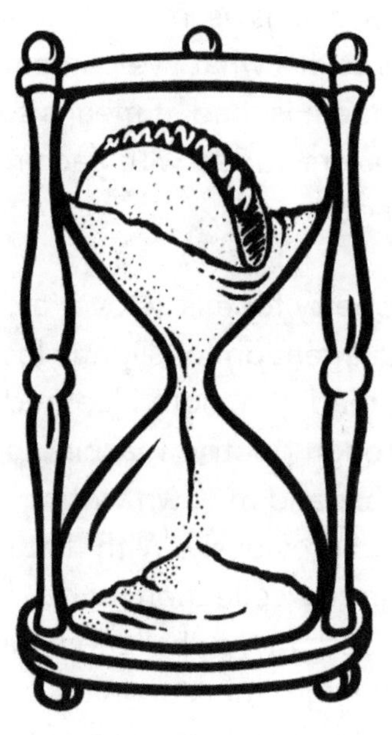

Contents

May I write words more naked than flesh,
stronger than bone,
more resilient than sinew,
sensitive than nerve.

~Sappho

All the while, believe me,
I prayed our night would last twice as long.

~Sappho

Tattoos, Tacos, and Time

Room for just one more;
Belly laughs over cheese dip;
We need more of this.

Fan

It's hot.
Sweat dripping into my eyes,
clothes clinging to my skin,
the ice in the lemonade
doesn't stand a chance,
kind of hot.
She sits on the porch swing,
sideways,
legs stretched long in front of her,
attempting to cool herself
with a fan she found
at an antique store,
eyes closed and head tossed back.
The way her neck exists, exposed
and then dips to find her shoulder,
I find the porch ceiling fan is insufficient
for cooling me off,
and it's not just the summer heat
I'm fighting.

Before

"Can I kiss you?"

"Yes."

Axis

That first kiss with her
shifted the world off
axis,
and we kept falling.

First Kiss

I close my eyes,
breathe you in
as you close the distance.
My exhale,
a sigh;
I feel you shudder,
your hand on my back
as warm as your smile.
Without speaking, absolute agreement -
this moment
is to be savored.
Barely touching
your lips brush mine;
brief pause,
impossibly holding back.
The electricity dancing,
anticipation singing,
willpower gone.
Mouths melting into
bliss,
softness,
sweetly connected,
fusion,
time no longer existing;
a world of our own,
possibility,
more than just a kiss.

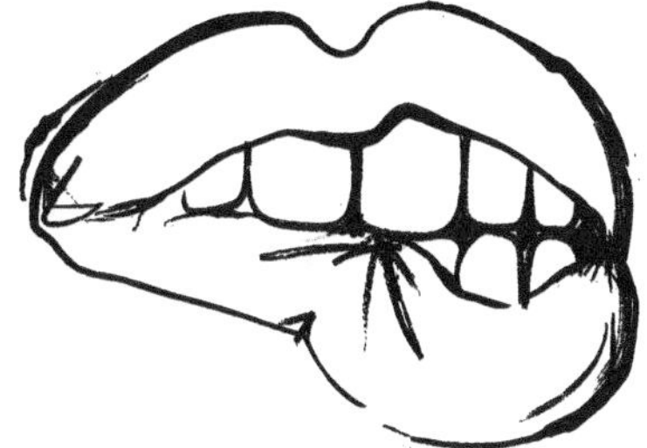

Button

Breaths hitch as my hands
Undo the button on your jeans, your
Teeth gently pulling my bottom lip and we're
Tangled up in sheets, skin to skin, the
"O" your mouth makes at my touch; we find
our rhythm and
Nothing feels as divine as these moments.

Starfish

One of my favorite memories of her?
She's laid out across the bed
like a starfish,
catching her breath,
my cheek laying against her
balmy, sweaty inner thigh.
We both sigh.

I Didn't Know

Things I didn't know
before I knew you:
a list turned poem, perhaps,
or just an acknowledgment,
an ode and testament to you,
to us.

Before you, I didn't know
that it was possible to love someone
so deeply, so intensely;
that love could feel like this.
I didn't know that
being in someone's presence
could feel like sunshine for my soul,
and that being apart felt cold and dark
as if the sun had gone behind the clouds,
and my heart, like the sun-deprived flower,
would shrink, feel like it was dying,
without its source of light.

I didn't know that my body
could react that way
at another's touch. That your touch
would feel so right and electric,
grounding me in moments with you;

that my body would crave
your hands on me,
your arms wrapped around me;
that your head on my chest
would feel like freedom,
not like being trapped or weighed down;
that we could laugh in the middle
of having sex, after the bed broke,
or any other time, and it would only
make us closer, make me want you more;
that love has a taste, and it's you, and
I crave it more than I knew possible.

I didn't know I could love someone
down to their fingertips,
the way their hands made letters
on paper, the sound and look
of their name. But then I met you.
And the simplest things
like a grocery list or a reminder note,
the sight of your name somewhere
evokes feelings -
physical, spiritual, emotional - that
overpower me, lack words to
adequately describe them,
overwhelm me in the best ways,
consume me.

I didn't know that bedtime routines
could feel so safe and cozy,
like a blanket wrapped around a long day;
that peace could feel like
quiet, routine, togetherness.
I didn't know showering with someone
could be erotic and familiar,
a way to care for you
as I wash your back, your hair,
another cherished time to talk about our days.
I didn't know I could feel so accepted
and beautiful standing naked before someone else
until your gaze held me securely
with a respectful, burning desire.

I didn't know that peanut butter sandwiches
taste better with cinnamon sprinkled atop them,
but of course they do;
or that so many small and helpless creatures
needed saving, placing off the main path,
yet I know this now.
I didn't know that I could lift more at the gym
than what I was doing;
you wouldn't let me settle,
so now I know I'm capable of so much more.
I didn't know that love
could make you want to be
a better person when you're with
the right person
who sees the person that you've been,
the person that you are, and
the person that you want to be.

I didn't know that you could say
"I love you" so many times
without it losing its meaning, its power,
without it getting "old".
I was afraid we'd grow tired of saying it
as often as we did, or that
it would lose its meaning and just be
words we expected to hear,
but that never happened, did it?
I didn't know that kissing someone
could feel divine,
take me out of time and place,
melt me further into you,
and be something I would think about
all the time,
that a first kiss could be so
magically haunting.

I didn't know that
trying to find the right damn words
to capture it all
could make me want to cry
because it's bigger
than anything I've ever known;
and so I don't yet have words
for exactly how this feels,
this love for you, this love.
I didn't know what love is
before I met you,
before you loved me,
before I loved you.

Devotion

Let me fall
to my knees before you
and worship
your body
for the masterpiece it is;
shaped by your adventures
seasoned with the delicacies you enjoy.
Let my tongue
whisper prayers of awe,
that you inspire,
over soft curves
and hard muscles,
my hands
find every sacred
part of you
and offer reverent
appreciation
well into the night
as the moon glows,
reflecting off your skin,
illuminating the hunger and
adoration-filled look
in our eyes
while we melt into
divine bliss,
filled with the kind
of devotion
that erases any doubts
about the way we feel
for each other.

Sensory

The cool, balmy feel of your inner thigh
as I lay my cheek against it,
having just feasted on you
I lay my head down on your leg
and smile in satisfaction and enjoyment.
The tangy sweet taste of you
the first time I lick you off my fingers
and my eyes roll back in my head
in delight at your deliciousness.
Wet and warm as I
slide my fingers inside you,
a new favorite place I like to be,
the softness of you there
transports me as close to heaven
as I've ever been since birth.
The smell of your skin,
I've said before,
is one I'd know anywhere;
distinctly you, and my favorite,
indescribable.
The touch of your hands
anywhere on my skin,
around my waist,
fingers interlocked,
twirling my hair;
I hated being touched
in any of those ways
before I felt your touch,
and now skin to skin with you
is my favorite way to exist.
Your fingers are calloused
from lifting and yet
make the slightest, softest whisper
of pressure across my skin

and despite the gentleness
I melt under it like it's full of fire.
The melody of your voice
is a song I play on repeat,
your laughter like magic and sunshine
and every good thing in the world,
and whether it's goofy voices
you give the dog or cat in conversation,
or the earnest and passionate sound
in your dreams and goals,
I'll wrap it around me every time,
a blanket of safety and care.
The sight of you moving,
cooking, getting dressed, running,
resting, concentrating, readying for bed,
are sights that captivate me.
I could watch you endlessly,
never grow tired,
and marvel at the way you
make your way
through the world.
You are a sensory experience
I cannot get enough of,
I never tire of,
and I miss when we're apart.
You are a sensory experience
words can never quite capture
in fullness
but that I sink into
every time I think of you.

Blindfold Me

Blindfold me
and I would know you still
by the feel of your body,
the strength of your muscles
and your curves, soft under my hands,
by your smell,
the intoxicating fragrance
of love and home,
and by your voice,
your laughter,
your whisper,
the sound of my name
on your lips and
the way "I love you" sounds
when you tell me how you feel;
by your energy,
the pull of your soul
drawing mine to you,
the feel of our connection
pulsing between us.

I could draw the shape of you
from memory,
recount the journey my hands take
each time I reach for your body,
the delicious dips
where your neck meets your shoulders,
your breasts meet in the middle
of your freckled chest,
the softest swells of beauty
dancing in my mind as I recall your form,
and your sides curve
as I find your hips,
and complimenting those sweet evocations

is the way my tongue adds details,
making sure the visual reproduction of you
in my reminiscing
takes my breath away as much as
you do in person, standing before me,
naked and beautiful.
Yes, demand a sketch
from memory only
and my senses will recreate you.

Blindfold me and my soul
will recognize my lover
and her love
without hesitation,
without question.
She is the one my soul knows
and it will know her in sight or without.

Lover

I call her lover
not only because she takes me to bed
and loves me well with a gentle touch
and a heat that burns through me,
consuming insecurity and anxiety,
leaving me worshiped
as I sink into blissful rest.

I call her lover
because she sees me
beyond the way I wear the years,
in ways no one before her has,
bare and vulnerable,
clothed in her desire.

I call her lover
because she knows
how I'm prone to worry and
the way I take my coffee,
knows me inside and out,
and loves each version of me,
even the in-between and
the ones she didn't know before we met
(I know this because she told me so).

I call her lover
because she carries my heart
like a delicate bud or
tender creature,
careful not to hurt or cause pain,
all the while also knowing
how tough, how strong it is.

I call her lover,
our souls pulled into each others' orbit,
her arms pulling me against her
our hearts connecting,
dreams colliding,
foreheads pressed together,
fingers entwined,
present flowing
into our future
becoming our present.

I call her lover.

There's Something About Her

Long day,
little fires,
missed deadlines,
another bill.
Irritating co-workers,
an overall sense of feeling uncomfortable;
forgot my lunch back at home,
spilled coffee everywhere.
Broken copier,
missed a turn,
traffic jam,
and I dropped
my arm full of papers
and watched them scatter.
The little things
can add up to feel
like the world is falling apart,
and even if the day was mid,
I'm feeling wound up and stressed.

There's something about her,
about that moment
when I see her smile and
get to hear her voice
for the first time that day.
And when she wraps me in her arms,
I feel my shoulders fall
and the breath I was holding
slips out in relief.
Peace comes as she
brushes hair from my face and
and I lay my head on her shoulder.
The world rebalances
the moment that she whispers
"It'll be alright".
Whatever the challenge I'm facing,
she's in my corner;
everything feels more doable,
easier to take on,
with her by my side.

I Will

I'll etch my memory
on your skin
like a poem
scribed for a lover.

Bury my taste
so deeply in your senses
that I spoil your appetite
for anyone else.

I'll hold you so often
and closely, safely,
that my touch feels like life support
and you will long not to be unplugged.

I'll plant my love
in the garden of your life
weeding out pain and negativity,
watch you unfurl and blossom.

I'll haunt your time when we're apart;
whispers of my voice tickling your ear,
the smell of me preventing you from forgetting,
phantom sensations along your skin
in my favorite places to touch you.

I'll pour my presence
so deeply in your soul
you'll wonder what life was like before me,
desire to name stars after me as a testament,
see me everywhere you go,
and finally know what it is to be truly loved.

Sometimes

Sometimes I look at you
and can't believe
I'm lucky enough
to get to love you;
that I get to hear
your dreams when they're still just ideas,
and am the one you choose to hold you
when the world goes sideways.

Sometimes I look at you
and marvel that
I've only known you
for a little while;
it feels like you know me more,
see me more clearly,
than anyone else
I've known longer.

Sometimes my stomach still does flips,
actually almost all the time,
when I think of you,
and when you kiss me,
each time you grab my hand to hold,
and when you say "I love you".

Sometimes I hold my breath
when you pull me close
because I'm afraid
to break the spell
of the moment. And
sometimes, when I least expect it,
you take my breath away;
but I don't miss it
because in exchange you've given me
a look, a smirk, a sigh,
little gestures that share big feelings.

Sometimes I can't stop myself,
from smiling at you or
grinning at a message you sent me,
or shake my head in disbelief
that somehow,
for some reason,
you aim your smile at me.

Sometimes I don't want
to wake up from this dream of us
until I remember that
all this love, these feelings, this connection
are not a fantasy,
that the way you say my name,
the way your body responds to my touch,
the fire you set within me,
is very much reality.

My Favorite Place

I can't say
I've been a lot of places,
but I have been
a few.

I've seen sunrises
crest the ocean horizon,
run on beaches
as golden rays shoot across
the lapping waves.

I've stood atop
mountains, gazing out
at breathtaking valleys,
magnificent green hillsides
spreading out like a blanket.

I've placed hands
on the whitest snow,
watched flakes flutter eagerly around me
towards the ground to coat
it in a sparkling iridescent magic.

I've gaped in awe
at art hung on gallery walls,
unraveling the story
artists attempted to tell us
in their paintings, sculptures, photographs.

I've closed my eyes and let
the beauty wash over me
at concerts and stared, wide-eyed
at the strength and grace of dancers
at ballets and recitals.

As amazing as these places have been,
as beautiful as they are in my memories,
none of them have reached the rank
of my favorite place.
Because my favorite place is

my head on her chest,
arm around her,
falling asleep in her arms;

riding shotgun,
radio playing, her hand in mine,
traveling anywhere together;

sitting across a table,
listening to her tell a story,
and watching her smile,

standing so close to her
I smell her (it smells like home),
and feel the warmth of her arms around me;

on a porch swing
next to her, listening to the sound
of night and our voices as fireflies dance;

stopping on the walk
with her to learn
what that flower is called,

any of the places
with everyday things,
as long as they
are with her.

Soft

I've always longed for
A soft place at the day's end
To land. I found you.🩶

Us

Words,
an hourglass
a countdown,
a definitive yet
currently undefined
ending point.
The tale's begun,
the story's unfolding
until it's time
to share it with the next one.

Actions,
a sunrise,
bringing warmth to the day,
a blanket wrapped securely,
offering comfort;
a summer night
full
of familiar smells,
fireflies dancing, glittering,
a marvelous joy
for the moment,
the present overflowing
with smiles and laughter.

Whispers, glances,
in between moments,
the ocean, rolling endlessly
out across the horizon;
the starry night sky
infinite possibilities,
always there, consistent,
even when hidden by daylight.
Like clouds at sunrise or sunset,
reaching,
stretching out to the future.

Time is wonderfully strange
when we're together;
present and future are
blended, simultaneous,
limited and endless,
known and still undiscovered,
sure and uncertain
a duality that is masterfully intertwined,
frighteningly vague and still taking shape,
comforting in these moments we're sharing,
the memories we're making.

I Crave You

I can't stop staring at you and the way you smile,

Curves covered in freckles hidden beneath
masculine clothes,
Raspy voice first thing in the morning
And when you're asking me not to stop,
Vulnerability and conversations about our dreams
draw me closer to you still,
Everything about you makes my stomach do flips
and leaves me

Yearning for your touch, your breath in my ear,
Or your lips pressed against mine, you are
Unequivocally all I think about and all I want.

Thinking of Her (Always)

Her smile makes me think
forever isn't that long;
rather, not enough.

Stand close behind me,
place a soft kiss on my neck;
watch me become hers.

Closed off to the world
I feel safe when I'm with her,
open as a book.

Intimate moments
as I share with her my past,
so vulnerable.

I don't fear judgment,
she loves me just as I am,
healing, not yet whole.

Flirty, spicy, sweet,
conversations between us
are always lively.

Inspiring me
to be my best everyday;
love, space when I'm not.

Take my breath away;
her eyes, her touch, and her kiss;
I'm endlessly hers.

Text Me

Poetry in Messages

You text and ask me how my morning's been.
I've made coffee that's it.
And daydreamed about annoying you
for the next 30 years.
This connection is unlike any other.

One time you joked
that feral creatures shouldn't be
domesticated. So I asked
Is it domestication if I can get
the feral one to eventually
go to bed and wake up with me
every day in the future?
Thankfully, you said it's not.
So... looking forward to all the nights
& all the mornings with you.

You've not been shy
about how you feel.
I've tried to tell you that
i have the same damn feelings
for you.
I hinted at the future
bc that's what I want.
It wasn't a hint,
it was as subtle
as a damn gunshot.

We both know you'll think through,
analyze, try to understand,
probably even overthink things.
I wish you'd trust what I say. But
I love you the way you are.
9478484 thoughts and all.

I felt like I had it all under control,
but you threw me for a loop.
I am so driven by you.
As cheesy as it might sound,
you & I
could change the world together.

And damnit, I wanna love you.
I love you and I know
that what you & I have
& can create together
is something bigger.
I have been in situations all week
where I have wanted to tell you
just how fucking much I love you
and I just didn't
because that's a big thing
and the last thing I want
is to scare you away.
Man… I am fucking smitten with you.

I cannot look at you and not see us.
It took us both by surprise,
It was never meant to be
more than a casual fling.
Yea, tbh it was allll fun in the beginning &
I can promise you that all the fun
I envisioned is now me tripping
over literally everything you say to me.

I want you to hear me.
I am crazy about you.
You're beautiful,
incredibly quirky in all the right ways,
emotionally, physically & mentally
just fucking strong. I admire that.
I admire you &
the way you move through this crazy world.
It's not easy at all, but somehow
you make it seem so simple.
Maybe it's just how I see you.
Like you could take over the world
& I'd be happy just to share
1 second with you.
Together we'll
Glow up and take over the world together.
You tell me you can't think of anything better....

I need you to trust me
whenever I tell you that I can't either.
And that will happen.

What you & I have is something
I've never really felt before
& I mean that.
What you & I talk about & share,
both emotionally, physically, etc.,
I don't have with anyone else.

And I think you're so fucking hot.
Like what the fuck.
Thinking about my hands
on your skin, kissing
your body, feeling you
relax into me...
All the fucking things that drive me crazy.
Now all I can think about
is you walking around
our house in my shirt
And there is
Nothing I wanna do more
than take my clothes off of you

You've sent another poem,
I swear I'll never get tired
of reading what you write.
Even when they're sad,
because
I like the way your brain works
And I like that
you share that part of you
with me.

I love you.
I honestly have
no other words
as to how I feel
about you.

Where you came from & where you're going.
Everything that made you who you are &
everything you wanna be in the future.
Every version of yourself
that you've given me the pleasure of knowing
& learning, I've loved.
I may not have been the first to love you,
But I'd like to be the last.

Craving

It's the way you get under my skin
and never out of my mind.
It's the way I wonder what
my name sounds like on your sigh,
and what your mouth tastes like
after you've begged for more.
It haunts me long past bedtime.
It's wondering how soft your touch is
or is it rough with longing need?
The way your fingertips imprint my skin
and leave it singing, pulsing, electric,
unsated and hungry.
And wondering how you can leave me craving
something I've not yet had.

Her, in Haiku

I want to trace the
freckles adorning her skin,
and kiss every one.

Green eyes I'm lost in;
captivating, magical,
take my breath away.

If she were a poem
her words would be solid, strong;
and her tone, sunshine.

Soft lips, two freckles,
knowing the way she tastes I'd
kiss her for hours .

Hard muscular lines,
soft curves - her breasts, hips, and ass;
together, divine.

She's easy to love,
healing herself, willing to
be vulnerable.

She's fire and love,
possesses passion and drive,
ignites my own flame.

There's pain from her past
that she doesn't succumb to;
choosing love instead.

There is depth to her -
intelligent, fine as hell,
humor, loves others.

Soul deep, passionate
conversations between us;
how we'll change the world.

Anytime with her
you can be sure we will laugh
until we're crying.

She moves through the world
with confidence, charm, and heart;
it makes her sexy.

Boots

Black dress, cut low in the front,
lace strap slipping off my shoulder,
silk hitting midway down my thighs,
eagerly waiting for your hands
to pull my knee-high boots off
then slide back up my legs;
My outfit tonight a spell I cast
to bring forth the magic you do so well.

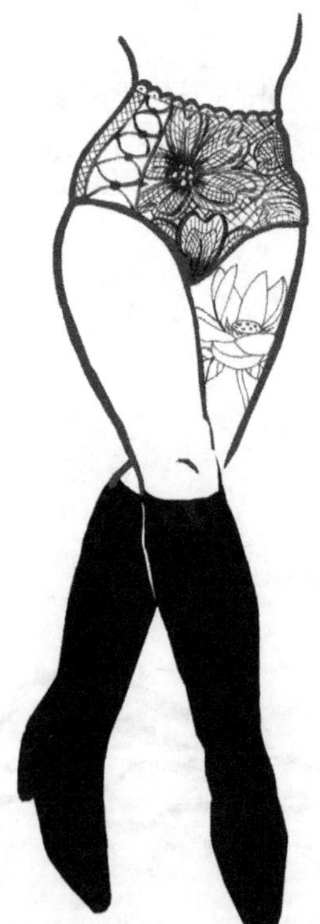

When I Say "I love you"

When I say "I love you"
I mean that I think
constantly of you;
my mind never seeks
to know another topic;
I see you everywhere
in everything.
There is always something
I think that you would like
or a story I want to share with you.

When I say "I love you"
I mean that you are
my safe space and
my soul finds peace with yours;
time with you is rest
and I don't have to be
anyone other than my most authentic self.
I know there is no judgment,
only love and support,
in your embrace of me.

When I say "I love you"
I mean that all of you
is precious to me;
every part of who you are matters,
including versions of yourself
before I knew you,
who you are on both
good days and bad ones.
Your demons cannot scare me;
I will love them, too.

When I say "I love you"
I mean that I can feel you
even when we're apart,
and I wish for you
a day that brings you happiness
until my arms can hold you again.
I carry you with me
in memories and laughter,
shared dreams and possibilities
for all that we can be.

When I say "I love you"
I mean that I will always
walk beside you
as you chase your dreams;
running hand in hand to reach them
and remind you of what you're after
should you forget or be discouraged.
I believe in you and all you bring
to everyone around us,
and count myself lucky to watch you change the world.

When I say "I love you"
I mean that you make me smile,
you make laughter bubble from my heart,
the same one you make skip a beat
when our eyes lock,
and you take my breath away,
no matter how much time has passed.
You make me want to dance,
and inspire me to always be
the best I can for this world.

When I say "I love you"
I mean that I am here,
here for you and whatever you may need.
I mean that I will keep learning
how to love you well,
and apologize when I misstep.
I mean that I will hold your heart
as carefully as my own,
as long as you'll allow it;
I'll love you endlessly.

Journal

I don't need a paper journal
to write my feelings in;
just give me your skin
and I'll record everything there.
I don't need a pen and ink
to mark my passions down;
I'll use my mouth, my tongue and teeth
to share this fire you ignite in me.
Written words are pretty;
they tell you how much I care,
and penned poems and essays
are lovely to re-read,
but I promise I will show you
precisely how much I love you
anytime you need.

Grungy

Grease and grass stains on overalls or
Ripped jeans and a thrifted tee
Understated outfits for hands-on work are her thing but
No one is as beautiful as she is, this
Girl takes my breath away and has me
Yearning for her to put those dirty hands on me.

This Girl

There's this girl who is
more beautiful than she knows;
who's eyes pull you under,
like quicksand,
into the depths of her.
She is brilliant,
and makes me laugh,
cares for herself
and others.
Gorgeous, with a clever mind
and a big heart,
is a dangerous combination.
And I am
d r a w n
to her.
It's an unnameable
connection,
an unexplainable
attraction,
a force so strong between us
there's no fighting it.
D r a w n
to her,
in ways I'm at a loss
to put words to.

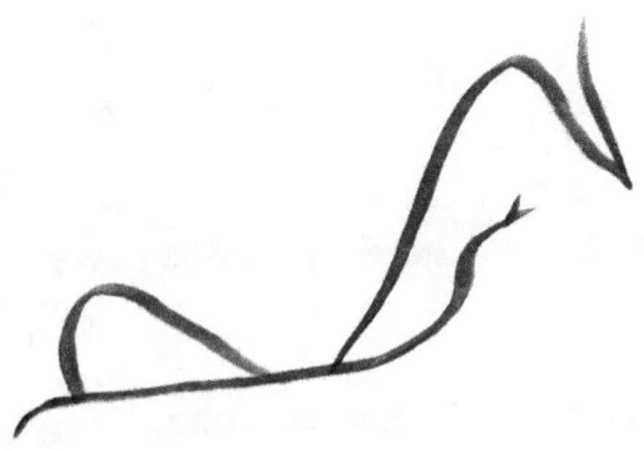

It's more than
a magnetic pull,
stronger than
the moon's hold
over the waves
and maybe that's why
I'm wet at her touch,
aching for her lips
on my neck, my mouth;
and maybe that's why
the way she covers
my body with her hands
makes me purr.
Perhaps it's also why,
when my fingers find their way
between her legs,
she's dripping,
wanting and ready
for me to love her,
and the way she feels
is exquisite.
Perhaps it explains
the way we melt,
two into one body,
my skin craving hers.
And certainly it's why
there's nothing I can do
about losing myself in her.

Contradictions

I can't catch my breath
when I'm near you
and all I want to do is breath you in,
that familiar smell
I would know anywhere.

My heart beat quickens
whenever you're close;
ironic because your presence
calms me in a way
I've never known.

Knees, weak at your proximity,
vibrating with anticipation;
I'm trying to stay standing,
as close to you as I can,
hoping our fingers brush.

Chill bumps pimple my skin,
a slight shiver at your touch
as electricity jumps through my veins
and your nearness warms me
from my soul out.

Sun

The sun pouring
through the sunroof as we drive
down a back road
on the way to somewhere together;
Sunlight reflecting off her sunglasses
as bright as the smile she flashes me,
while she laces her fingers with mine;
Sunshine across her skin
as she lays in bed with a
sleepy grin and tussled hair,
a lazy start to our day.
The way she brightens
gray and gloomy days
with encouragement and love
and holds space for my worries
while supporting my dreams,
like the sun slipping out from behind dark clouds.
The way the space around me
goes cold when I leave her presence
and the warmth of her gone;
the way night air chills
once the sun has set.
Like Icarus to the sun,
I'm drawn to her.

With You

I want to fill my days with you;
lazy days
snuggled on the couch
in front of an old movie
or napping, tangled up together
under a blanket.
I want to fill my days with you;
long drives
to new experiences and sights,
wrong turns just to make it
more exciting.
I want to fill my days with you;
changing the world
dreaming and building and
making safe spaces for others;
reaching our goals
together.
I want to fill my days with you;
birthdays and occasions,
holidays and just because days,
days that are special only
to us, no one else, because they're spent
together.

I want to fill my days with you;
appreciating
your smile, your laugh, your passion,
your body, your mind, your heart,
everything about you that makes you unique.
I want to fill my days with you;
until we no longer can,
until our love has faded,
or age has grayed our hair,
until you don't find me
to be full of a magic that
calls to you.
I want to
fill my days
with you.

Exotic

Some people long for
far away places
with white sand beaches,
crystal clear skies,
bottomless blue oceans.
Some people ache to go
explore rainforests,
climb mountains,
dive deep into oceans, and
discover uncharted trails.
And while those adventures
would undoubtedly be amazing,
I crave a different sort
of everyday adventure.
I desire to explore her body,
and all its muscular lines and soft curves.
to trace the freckles on her skin
that number as many as the grains of sand;
I hope to climb the walls of her heart
and tear down any fear and insecurity there,
making it crystal clear
my intentions with her are pure;
let me get lost in her eyes,
those bottomless pools
of magic and mischief,
and dive deep into her soul as I
find a place for mine to land.
I will discover her dreams and
together we'll map a way
to change the world.
Because her love is all the exotic that I need.

Home

If home isn't
a place,
or rather
is any place so long
as certain aspects
also exist there -
feelings, people,
experiences, moments -
then home is
the smell of
meals cooked with
love and laughter
mixed with
the smell of her skin
after a shower,
when she first wakes up, and
after she's been well loved;
the smell of home is
one I'd know anywhere.

Home is a safe place to land
at the end of a hard day,
her shoulder to
lay my head on,
her arms wrapped around me,
holding my
pain, sadness, exhaustion,
her smile celebrating
my joy, my wins.

Home is her allowing me
to carry her struggles
as if they are my own,
her sinking into
the comfort my heart
longs to offer her.

Home is each of us
protecting the other,
taking care together,
us against the world.

Home is the sound
of laughter,
hers my favorite song,
a melody I carry with me
out into the world,
mine more frequent
in her presence.

Home is flirting,
no matter how long
we've been together;
an art, our banter,
both sweet and spicy words,
sultry looks, and
simple brushes of our bodies
against each other
through the day.

Home is a place
to speak dreams and hopes
and knowing they are safe,
they are cherished,
and there is room to grow
together.

Home is knowing
when we need solitude,
time to restore ourselves,
and though we spend
that time apart,
we carry home with us
in our hearts.

Home is
laying down at night
next to a woman
who loves me as big as
I love her.
Whispered affections,
sensual touches,
listening to her breathe;
my head on her chest,
her arms around me,
soft, together,
in each other's peace.

Home is a place
I've yet been,
but I have glimpsed.
Home is a place
I'm still searching to find,
a place I'm longing to go,
to know,
to have.

Let Me Know

Write me love notes
and let me know
you're thinking of me
when we're not together,
and watch my face
light up when you
hand them to me
or hide them in places
to surprise me;
Kiss the top of my hand
after you interlock our fingers,
pulling me in close as you do,
because you know
one of my favorite places
is tucked into your arms.
Send me things
that made you think of me -
a song, a picture, a meme -
pick a flower you see
growing wildly somewhere
that makes you think of me,
or a rock on your walk
who's shape or color brings me to mind,
give me trinkets and images
to collect and hold on to
when we can't be together,
that make me think of you
more often than I already do
(which is nearly all the time).
Don't be afraid to say

how you feel;
let me know
where I stand,
tell me often
what you think of
when you think of me
and let it all feel like
it's unique to us,
not the same ways
you loved someone else, but
gestures that reflect
how special what we have is
and how different it is
from any other relationships.
Love me quietly when we're alone,
love me loudly when we're not;
love me the same no matter
whose company we're in.
Don't let me forget
what I mean to you;
don't assume I know.

Childhood Friends

Is it strange
that sometimes, when you tell me
a story from your childhood,
that I long
to have known you then
and wish that
we were friends
so I could
stand up for you,
comfort you,
make you laugh
instead of cry,
and we could
plot revenge
and giggle about silly things
until you didn't hurt anymore?

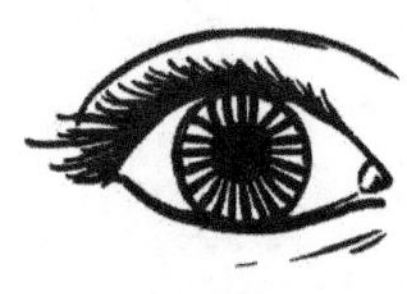

Is it odd
that when you share
how you felt
when you were younger
in some situation or other
that left you scared
or lonely,
unsure or sad,
I ache to have been there
to have been able
to hold you
until the feelings passed?

We weren't childhood friends,
grew up in different cities,
didn't meet until we were adults,
but that doesn't stop this feeling.
I'm glad I know you now;
please know that I will hold,
not only you in my arms,
when life gets hard
and choices are tough;
I'll also hold your inner child
tight within my love.

The younger you who still peers out
from deep inside your soul,
I see her beauty,
it's there behind your eyes,
and her sparkle shines brightly
every time you smile.

So, my love, please know
you are safe,
and so is she,
as long as I am here.

Boring

When you say boring,
do you mean morning coffee
on the weekends
with your favorite person?

When you say boring,
do you mean listening to
rain outside, the door propped open
while we sit side by side on the couch?

When you say boring,
do you mean cooking
our favorite meal together,
laughing and dancing
and eventually getting dinner ready?

When you say boring,
do you mean porch-swinging
as the sun goes down
and the fireflies twinkle?

When you say boring,
do you mean slow walks
through the woods,
stopping to spy the wildlife
and see what flowers decorate the trail?

When you say boring,
do you mean holding hands
while we drive somewhere,
anywhere,
taking the long way there?

When you say boring,
do you mean laying my head
on your chest
as we lay down at night
and you pull me close?

When you say boring,
do you mean laying
your head in my lap,
letting me run my fingers
through your hair and place
a kiss on your forehead
before whispering
"I love you"?

When you say boring,
do you mean long naps,
belly laughs,
stolen kisses,
knowing glances,
inside jokes,
shared dreams,
deep talks,
watching reruns,
figuring it out,
love notes,
doing dishes together,
ass smacks,
kisses at red lights and stop signs,
and a million other everyday things?

Because if you mean those things,
the simple things
the simple pleasures
the simple joys
the simple moments
then, baby, bore me to death,
because all I want
is a simple life
with you.

When

When I read
words of a poem,
lines from a story,
it doesn't have to be
about you
for me to think of you.

When I visit a place
and hear a song,
see something beautiful
and have my breath taken away,
it doesn't have to be
a place we've been
or a song we've heard,
even an experience together
for me to think of you.

When I think of
the history
that made us who we are,
that taught us how to be,
that nurtured our roots,
it doesn't have to be
a shared one
for me to know it brought
us to this moment.

When I dance in the rain
or the kitchen,
and smile at the sound
of you laughing at my silliness,
it doesn't have to be from the other room
to make me long for you
to join me.

When I close my eyes
I don't have to have your face
memorized
to see you
in my dreams.

Work of Art

She decorates her home
with trinkets from
travels and wanderings
to remind her
of the places she's been
and where she plans to return.
I like to hear about them all.

She decorates her body
with inked stories,
both fantasy and
memory, in black and gray
and color;
I love learning more about her
as she explains each one.

She decorates her heart
with treasures
from loved ones and friendships,
marking struggles overcome,
achievements won, celebrations;
I add them to my own
cherished things because I treasure her.

And while she collects
and expands the ways she
decorates her life,
she overlooks, forgets, ignores
the way others decorate their lives
with her presence and smile,
her laugh, her intellect,
her joy and her passion,
because she is a work of art.

Weave

Go beyond bone deep,
skin to skin is not enough;
weave your soul with mine.

Heavy

Holding each other up when
Everything seems to be falling down
And standing together against the world,
Vital to the bond that endlessly holds them
  together.
Yes, love makes life less heavy.

Loving You

Loving you scares me
in the way that not
knowing where I'm going or
not having directions does when
I'm desperately trying to get somewhere
important.

Loving you excites me
like a new adventure
I'm packing for, planning for, preparing for,
knowing there are so many possibilities
and the best part is
all the parts I don't know yet
and cannot control.

Loving you scares me
like wanting a particular outcome
in a game or project or situation
where I don't have control
over anything but my part.

Loving you makes my heart
beat fast and full
like stepping into something
I've wanted for so long and
am finally getting to experience.

Loving you scares me like
learning something new
but exciting because
I want to do it well.

Loving you calms me
like the familiar smells
of home and sounds of
comfort emanating from
favorite places.

Loving you scares me
because what if I mess up?
What if I leave something unsaid,
don't tell you how incredible you are,
leave you wondering where
you stand with me or how much
you have of my heart?

Loving you inspires me to give
the best of myself and to be
the best me I can,
to keep trying when I don't know
and to take risks I did not
believe possible but know
are safe with you.

Loving you scares me
as I try to love you well
and cherish you, being gentle
with your pain and past
and not leaving things unsaid;
holding you close and leaving
you room to breathe and be.

Loving you is as beautiful as
the sparkle in your eyes
that brings a smile to my face,
the breath in my lungs
that you take away,
the softness of your hands in mine
that remind me I'm not in this alone.
Loving you is the wildest adventure
I never knew I'd need
but always believed I deserved.

Never Enough

There are always more words
on my mind,
in my heart,
than I can get on paper
(or typed in my notes app),
captured in verse.

More words I want to tell her
so she knows
how I feel,
how much I care,
my fears,
my hopes
for us.

I think my mind stumbles
on how big the feelings are,
how much they still
take me by surprise.
Or maybe it's the way
I wander into worrying
that it's all too good
to be true
or that I'm imagining
there's more there than really is.
Or that I'll run out of time
to tell her, show her, let her know
because sometimes I can't even
find the words I need
to make her understand.

I love her name
as much as my own;
the way it sounds
when I speak it aloud,
when I whisper it softly;
the way it looks
on my phone screen when she calls
or as a notification when she texts,
and when I write it next to mine.

I love the possibility
of what we can do together in this world,
of all the ways we'll change it,
ten toes down, to steal her phrase;
But it's true, isn't it?
I've never felt so sure.

I love
the energy between us,
the pull of our hearts,
our souls,
magnetic and strong,
drawing me back to her always.

And once again
I'll pen this poem
and know it comes up short;
no matter how long I write,
how much I say,
it will never be enough
to do justice to this way
that I love her.

Home is Her

Rain falls on the tin roof,
tapping out a rhythm
that mimics our region's slow drawl;
she's on the front porch,
barefoot, blue jeans, bright eyed,
wearing my Panther's T-shirt,
wet hair, coffee mug in hand.
I sit down next to her,
lay my head on her shoulder
as she leans into me;
we listen,
breathe in the scent of wet leaves,
and freshly mowed grass.
The dogs lay still at our feet,
while lightning bugs
dance across the yard;
thunder rumbles in the distance,
a reminder of the passing storm,
the wind whispering softly
through the pine trees.
Even if life takes us east across the state
or westward across the country,
our song will always be this,
the sound of summer in the south,
and my home will always be
here with her.

Sweep

Stay a while with me.
We'll build a life and chase our dreams,
Explore the world together, and also
Enjoy mundane everyday things,
Put dishes away, sweep the floor, watch fireflies,
and make memories.

Memory Lane

We're sitting at lunch,
or maybe it's dinner,
at a Mexican restaurant
we frequent.
I don't recall
what prompted the trip
down memory lane,
but somehow we agreed
to take the walk;
so we grabbed hands
and started out together.
We spent at least an hour
going through old texts,
cringing at the cringy parts,
laughing at our past selves
as we read back over
those first conversations.
"I can't believe I said that"
and
"Wow, that was cheesy."
and
"Wait! Listen to this one."
Line after line,
message after message,
we wound our way back
from the beginning
to that present moment
sitting across from each other
in the booth at a Mexican restaurant,
a bowl of salsa
and a basket of chips between us,
more in love than either of us
knew we'd be.

Jealous

I spoke to the stars about her,
as they twinkled over Brown Mountain,
and they told me
they're jealous of her eyes
and the way they sparkle.

I spoke to the wind about her,
as it blew through the trees
on the mountain trails,
and it whispered solemnly
that it envies how gentle her touch is,
and in contrast, how strong her will is.

I spoke to the sunlight about her
as it made its way across the sky
to settle in the evening here in the west,
and it confessed
that it longed to shine as brightly
as her smile when it lights up a room.

I spoke to the ocean about her,
and in each rhythmic wave
lapping against the shore,
it confided it is jealous
of the depths of her empathy.

I spoke to the songbirds about her
and in between their morning melodies
and evening serenades,
they told me they are jealous
of the way her laugh is a song unmatched.

I spoke to the winding river about her
and as it made its way along its course,
over mountain rock beds and
through the shaded woods,
nurturing plants and creatures all,
it shared with me it's jealous of her
and the endless way
she takes care of those she loves.

I spoke to the mountains about her
and as they stood stalwart along the Blue Ridge,
they told me of their jealousy
for her strength,
the way she holds up so many.

I spoke to the universe about her,
and she was not surprised to hear
that I found her in everything I saw,
and that everywhere I mentioned her,
I found my audience in awe;
she is a woman after all.

What cannot be said will be wept.

~Sappho

Paper Dreams

What do I do
with dreams that can't come true?
When the daydreams
turned hoped-for
real-life happenings
no longer have the chance
to be?
I guess I can put them here,
on paper,
maybe something delicate,
or fancy,
and let them unfurl
in cursive script
so they have the same feel
of importance and substance
as they used to in my heart.
I'll hang them here
on paper,
like delicate art,
give them a life they can't have now.

I'll talk about
the cozy warmth
that was going to be
a home for us,
dinners at night,
made with love and laughter,
traditions created,
walls showcasing our adventures.
In bold, firm letters
describe the solid walls
that held us safe
allowed us to break down
the walls between us and
be vulnerable and soft.
I'll color in the dancing,
the touches when we pass
each other in any space,
life giving
like the green and vining plants
we care for as tenderly
as we do each other.
I guess when dreams can't come true
it's necessary
to write them down,
fold the paper
like a love note,
and store them
in that box of treasures
that also holds
the memories of us.

Waiting

To wait (v): stay where one is or delay action until a particular time or until something else happens

I know things may change
the more time that goes by;
it's only been a short time now
but still…
I'd wait. If you asked me to,
I'd wait for you.

Endless Grief

Every day my heart
wakes up and thinks it could be
different someday.

And each time my brain
reminds my little foolish heart
that no, it won't be.

So I greet new days
with fresh tears and with new grief,
losing you each time.

Memory Lane - Reprise

Now I can sit anywhere
and memories overtake me,
it doesn't matter how fast
I've tried to outrun them.
It's not that I mind
thinking of you, of us;
I love those reminders, actually,
that I was loved,
that I mattered once to you.
The hardest part these days
is that instead of reminiscing
together over a basket of chips
and laughing over queso,
I'm wandering memory lane alone.

All It Took

All I ever wanted
was to make your life easier
and more joyful.
I wonder now,
that you don't have to think of me,
if that's all it took after all.

Turn Off

When thoughts turn to you
I crave a drink of whiskey
to try to go numb.

I pledged that I'd stop;
didn't like losing myself
to the void like that.

They say distraction
is actually not best;
don't avoid feelings.

Even a geyser
or volcanic eruption
will pause sometimes.

I still can't seem to
find a way to turn them off -
feelings, brain, or heart.

Don't Be Sad

Don't be sad, you said.
A flower wilts without sun,
life cold in the dark.
Don't be sad, you said.
You have no idea how much
I wish I wasn't.

Foolish

I fin'ly let go,
believed the future you spun.
Then you walked away.

Haunting

I hope I haunt you,
memories and what if's,
the way you haunt me.

Too Good

Bound to happen or
self fulfilling prophecy?
Too good to be true.

Secret Third Thing

I wish she had known
it needn't be forever,
just a 'lil longer.

Drink

No longer can I
Quench my thirst at her thighs, so
I'll drink the moonbeams. 🌕

My Mistake

I took for granted
her telling me I'm pretty.
Now I tell myself.

I took for granted
hearing her say "I love you".
If only, once more...

I took for granted
we'd see the world together.
Ticket for one, please.

I took for granted
the way she spoke of one day.
Endlessly found end.

I took for granted
all the words she spoke were true.
That was my mistake.

Sting

Knowing I could not
be enough for you to stay?
It stings endlessly.

Sting II

I hope knowing that
my love was more than enough
is an endless sting.

Onion

Standing by the stove
where I once cooked her dinner,
onions make me cry.

Pierce

Promises spoken
in laughter, connection, words;
shattered dreams pierce sharp.

Absence

The evening sun
lands warm across my face
turning my cheek pink;
it is golden light in the sky,
reaching down,
nourishing the green leaves,
the emerald blades of grass
the autumn flowers.
And still it pales
in comparison to
the sunshine of your soul
the warmth of your arms around me
the way your laugh nurtures my joy
and pours light into my soul.
In your absence,
I'll sit a while outside
and hope the sun
will be a sufficient replacement
for now.

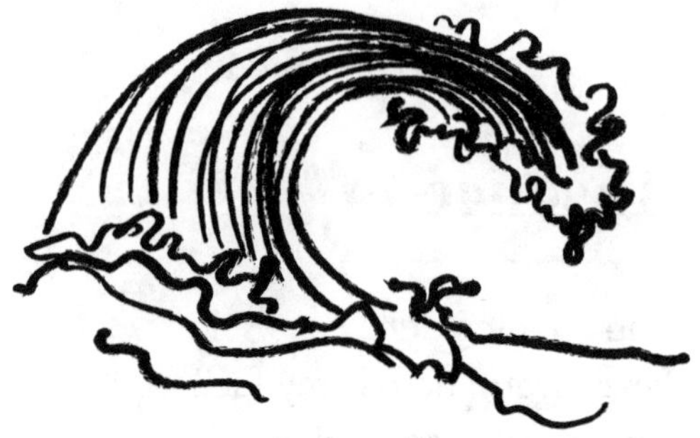

Grief

Gone. Just like that. Gone.

Running scenarios through my mind to see what
could've changed things

I hate the way the waves come and pull me under
without warning, leaving me drowning but never dead

Enough unanswered questions to last a
lifetime in multiple universes

Finding that I'm stronger than I want to be
simply because I have to be.

Let Me

Pain and hurt emanate from you,
anger, too;
they have stolen
the sparkle from your eyes
the laughter from your voice
the tenderness from your touch
the gentleness of your words;
I can see that it is all justified,
the ache, the anguish,
the fire that burns you up right now.

And because I love you,
my heart opens its door to you
and pain squeezes tightly
clamping closed wretched fingers,
chokes my words, my thoughts, and
applies pressure
until tears spring to my eyes.
I ache with sadness for you, not pity,
with a desire to make your world right again.
I am angry, too, on your behalf,
angry at the world that has hurt you,
but I know
it is not mine to take away.

Your pain is not something
I can take up a sword against and
cut down like overgrown weeds
no matter how deeply I long to do so.
Your hurting is not mine to
wipe away like I can the tears
that race down your cheeks
even though I ache to be able to.
Your anger is not mine
to slay or soothe or soften.
And yet…

I can hold it
for a time, a moment or more,
and give you rest,
allow you space to renew your fight.
I can carry some of your pain
and let you catch your breath,
give you time to start healing
before taking on the entire hurt.
I can walk with you
so you don't have to be alone
in facing the darkness.
I can show you your light,
remind you of your strength,
point to all the good in you,
hold up a mirror so you can see
what you've already handled.
You only have to allow me;
to let me in.

Truth

Is something true
because the speaker believes it to be
or is it true because
the hearer believes it so?

Does something become truth
the moment it happens,
is backed up by action
or can a sentiment be true
simply when it is spoken?

Are intentions truth
or do they require follow up,
follow through?

If a promise is broken
when the words aren't followed
by the actual thing promised
does that mean it was never true?

Or was it true in a way
in that in between space
when someone meant it and spoke it
before they realized it was more
than they could keep?

How long do you wait
from spoken to fulfilled
before something is deemed
no longer true?
Do you wait a lifetime?
Is it always true
as long as someone is still
waiting and hoping for it
to be so?

How do I know
what is true
when the monsters in my brain
are set on breaking my heart,
pinpointing all the things
that could be questioned?
How does one recognize
truth?

I Miss...

The way she used to
meet me at the door like
she had been waiting on me
so long and couldn't wait
a moment more;
Cooking in her kitchen
while she interrupted
every chance she could
so that it took twice as long
to make our meal,
And the way she put her arms
around me from behind
and kissed my neck;
At least the interruptions
were as delicious as the food.
I miss...
Sleepovers,
staying up late
talking about anything
and everything
before tucking in next to her
her arms tight around me,
the sound of her breathing
soft in my ear;
Dates, and holding hands
in public places

even if it was in the dark
or under the table,
walking with her arm around me,
feeling how very much she was
proud to be with me.
I miss…
Our snarky banter (flirting)
and building that spicy energy
between us
then finally releasing
all that delicious tension
through eager hands on bare skin,
kisses, moans, and whispers,
building a different kind of heat
before collapsing, naked,
in each others arms.
I miss…
Hope for a future for us
that was never really
talked about but always
hinted at, texts that implied
more time than
it sometimes seems we had;
Thinking there was a chance
one day I could call her mine,
and hearing her say to me
"I'm not going anywhere",
even if it was a lie.
I miss…
Making out and
dinner dates and
meaningful looks across a room,
Messages from her
about how much she thinks of me
and all the times she's missing me.

The Next Day

I'm watching the sunrise
with only memories of you;
it was supposed to be
with you by my side,
arms wrapped around me,
chin tucked into my neck

I'm watching a new day
open with opportunity;
instead of greeting it with you
I'm grieving it without you
breathing sweetly
next to me

I'm watching the next day
after losing you
show up unbothered,
not giving me
time to be sad,
demanding I keep going
when I don't have the heart,
because it was supposed to be
another day
I walked into hand in hand with
you
but all I've got to hold now
are memories and broken
dreams.

Remote

Realizing
Everything she said had a double
Meaning, like a story has two sides
Only I hoped for one thing
To find out she meant the opposite
Explaining the remote chance I ever had of
her loving me.

Cringy Cliches to Cling To

(When You Feel Like You're Falling Apart)

"Absence makes the heart grow fonder"
I can guarantee, from personal experience,
that the absence of love,
the absence of the warm touch of another,
the absence of affirmations,
tight hugs, conspiring smiles, and raucous laughter,
the absence of these things indeed
makes the heart grow fonder for them,
long for them,
ache for them.
But fondness doesn't fill an empty heart.

"Everything happens for a reason"
The challenge here is
you'll always wonder at the reason.
And the more you try to figure it out,
because why wouldn't you? Isn't
this platitude meant to reassure you?
And what can be more reassuring than knowing, than answers?
The more you try to figure it out
the less reasoned your thinking becomes,
the more desperate to know you are,
and the further from understanding you get.
Because maybe all it really is
is a fancy way to describe cause and effect,
or that physics law about
every action having an equal and opposite reaction.

"This too shall pass"
Pass by?
Pass over?
Pass away?
Can I pass it off to someone else to deal with?
Can you promise me that when it passes
I'll like the outcome, the resolution?
Because if there's the slightest chance
I could influence what happens,
turn the tide in my favor,
I'm not ready for it to pass just yet.

"You made your bed; now you have to lie in it"
This one amuses me
because I've never been one
to make my bed with any regularity,
so it's funny that my metaphorical bed
would be any different,
meaning maybe I should go about my life
with a little more intention and purpose.
Maybe then I wouldn't mind laying in
a bed I made of soft words,
grace for myself,
love,
and maybe then,
with a metaphorical bed well made,
my actual bed wouldn't feel so lonely.

Perhaps cliches aren't
what I'm looking for at all....

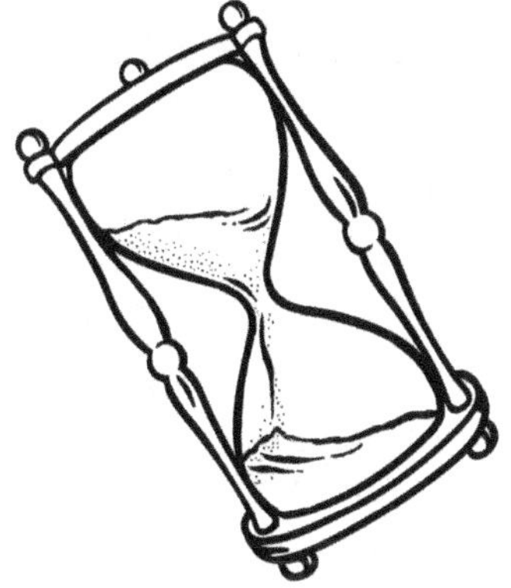

Take It Back

Take back the way you smiled at me
that made me weak in the knees
and caused my heart to skip a beat;
Take back the sweet words you said
that made me fall so fast
and left me longing for more of your
affection;
Take back the soft caress you used
to break down my stubborn walls
the one you used to fling wide
the rusted gate to my soul;
take back the whispered promises
that I collected and stored up
and played on repeat in my mind on the
tough days.
Take it all back and let me forget,
let memories unwind
because surely the pain of never knowing
hurts less than losing....

Nightmare

I want to scream
as the pain
tears apart my heart,
sadness seeping into the spaces,
scream as my soul
breaks free from my body,
scream until the universe hears
my suffering.
I want to pound my fists
against your chest and cry,
tear-stained face begging
tell me why,
pound my fists against your chest
and demand to know
why you're so stoic,
unbothered.
I want to sob into your shoulder
as you hold me close, tightly
wrapping me up in a familiar way,
always calming my tides.
Sob into your shoulder
as I fight to make sense
of something that seems unknowable.

I want to whisper
into your ear
how much I will always
love you and the time we shared,
whisper into your memory
some piece of me
that you can never dislodge,
that you will always carry.
I want to wake up
smiling next to you
as you wipe away a tear from my cheek,
along with the nightmare,
that I was losing you,
wake up next to you
smiling back at me
as you remind me you're right here
and you're not going anywhere.

Wanted...

A woman who
loves me as big as I love her,
a hopeless romantic
who leaves love notes
for me to find.
I don't need a romance story style
grand gesture,
consistent small ones will do;
Simply lets me know how she feels,
what I mean to her.
A woman who dances
in the kitchen with me
while I cook for us,
a woman who is playful
and makes me laugh,
but knows when to be serious.
A woman who can express
her feelings and desires,
who knows how to ask for
what she needs from me,
Someone who isn't afraid
to be vulnerable or cry,
who makes sure I never wonder
what I am to her.
A woman seeking adventures,
always ready to go somewhere,
as long as it's the two of us,
it doesn't matter where,
the "yes"on her lips
before I finish asking.

A woman who likes to plan
surprises, just to see me smile,
a date, a trip, or something
much more simple.
Someone who I can lean on
and talk to when the day is tough
and who, in turn, will let me
help hold her burdens, too.
A dreamer,
a world changer,
a bleeding heart like me,
trustworthy, loyal, loves to dote
and shower me with affection,
but lets me do the same for her.
My biggest fan, and
someone who sees me as enough
every time she looks at me.
My heart is hers, and hers is mine;
the only souls we want
are each others'.
Wanted:
My person, my next adventure,
my love.
Where are you?
When will I find you?
Do you know you're wanted?
Does my longing heart
beat a rhythm that you know
that calls to you and leads you
home to me?

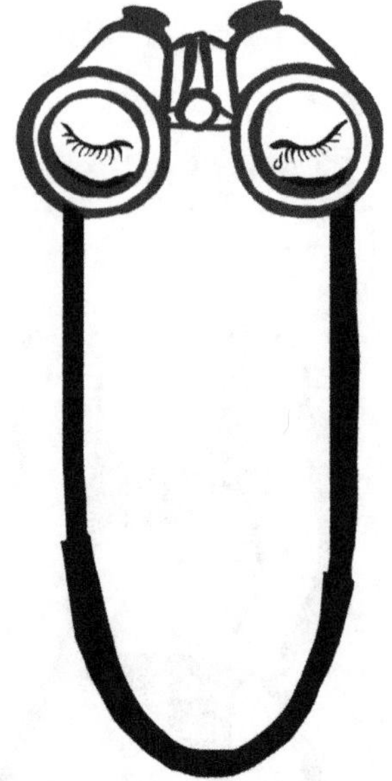

Binoculars

We had a pair of binoculars once
when I was a child.
They were fascinating,
allowing us to see
an entire world around us
as if it were closer than it was.
Sometimes I wish I had
emotional binoculars,
now, as an adult
so that my heart could pretend
you're closer than you are.

Backpack

It stays at the ready,
my backpack,
to help me make
that quick escape
when I'm feeling unloveable,
unworthy, not enough;
when things don't make sense
and answers aren't
apparent;
to help me flee
when emotions grow big,
and I'm afraid of getting hurt,
having my heart broken,
and it's easier to leave
than navigate the depths
of pain.
My backpack isn't made
for swimming after all,
even the metaphorical kind.

It stays half packed,
my backpack,
because that's easier
to maintain
than it is to hide
the disappointment from
being unknown, unseen,
misunderstood,
again.

But my backpack is worn,
a hole forming at the seam,
one strap fraying,
a zipper coming unstitched,
tougher to carry each time I pick it up,
every time I stuff it full
and make to move on.
Each time I unpack it a little,
to try to stay,
to want to have someone
know me, love me, see me,
it becomes a little more worn,
just like my heart.

Hope is a heavy thing,
weighing me down,
as I silently plead
to finally be able to
empty my backpack
and stay.

Confessions

I hope you think of me
every moment you're with her,
that
nothing she says
makes you laugh as hard
as when we're together,
and your words
are by far less charming
when she's your audience.
I hope my scent haunts you
the closer you get to her,
reminding you
of every time you
pull me near and say "I love
you",
that the taste of me
ruins your appetite
for her, and anyone else.
I hope the feel of her skin
brings tears to your eyes
and a longing to your heart
to have your hands on me,
and that when she touches you
it feels empty and cold,
your body is filled
with desire for the way
I make you feel.

I hope my name
escapes your lips
when you're dreaming,
asleep in her bed.
And when you daydream, that
I'm the only one you see,
the only one you want,
the only love you know.

I Fell

I fell into friendship
with a girl I met;
an unexpected but not
unwelcomed
kind of friendship.

A never laughed so hard
or felt as inspired to be
the best version of me,
fiercely supporting each other's
dreams
kind of friendship

A "here try this",
"I thought of you when",
share a joke, a meme, a song,
"I've got extra",
first person I think of
when there's an adventure
kind of friendship.

A checks in on me,
"Have you eaten?",
"Did you sleep well?",
"How's your day been?",
kind of friendship.

The kind of comfortable
you get from a lifetime of
experiences
and knowing someone
as well as you know yourself,
in less than a lifetime's time
kind of friendship.

I fell in love
with a good friend,
head over heels
crazy about her,
always on my mind
kind of love.

A can't get enough,
spend every chance I can
in her orbit,
even in silence
in the same space,
kind of love.

A make you think about
things you've never thought about,
wild dreams,
possibilities,
kind of love.

A sparks fly,
get lost in her eyes,
daydream,
nighttime dreams,
kind of love.

The unexplainable kind,
know it deep down,
soul connection,
everyone thinks you're crazy
kind of love.

She's in love with another girl,
and I'm lucky,
I guess,
when I can ignore it.
And I'll be grateful
for every moment
as friends that
we still share;
yes, it's a good thing
I fell into friendship
with her, too.

Whatever one loves most is beautiful.

~Sappho

Guidebook

Flip through the pages;
randomly we'll choose the trip,
our next adventure.

Roam

No destination,
we set out together to
see where life takes us.

Snacks

Intimate knowledge,
to know your favorite snacks
and ready them for the trip.

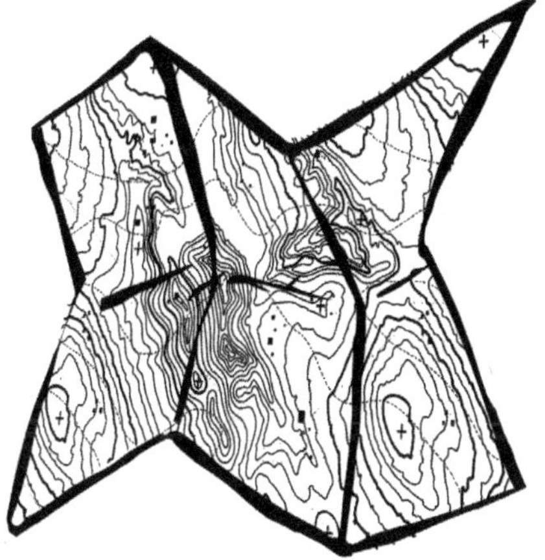

Horizon

With you anywhere,
sun sinking down, rising again,
our new beginnings.

Passport

Stamps placed on paper,
kisses in gorgeous places;
everywhere with you.

Hike

Heading into the woods together,
I close my eyes and open my soul
Knocking on the door of ancient energy
Enchanted once again.

Collections

When I was a babe
I collected affections,
kisses and snuggles
and adoration.

When I was a child,
I collected rocks
and sticks and leaves,
time outdoors.
Treasures Mother Earth
set out for me to find.

When I was a teen,
I collected expectations,
roles I should fill
and jobs I should hold,
things I should grow up to be.

When I was a youth
I collected ideas,
right and wrong,
of the way the world would
see me.

Now, as an adult,
I collect pieces
of a broken heart,
of shattered dreams,
of ceilings broken,
of expectations destroyed.
And I choose which ones
I will put back together
and carry with me.

To My Younger Self

I see you,
running wild and free,
imagination taking the lead,
demanding to know why boys
can go shirtless but girls
cannot;
sitting in the retro lawn chair
knees bent and legs spread,
a quarter of a watermelon in the space between,
juice running down your chin and arms;
they tell you to sit more ladylike
and you don't budge.

I see you,
huddled in a corner
of the bedroom with your siblings,
telling them it will be okay
as the soundtrack of
your parents' arguing plays on repeat;
learning through watching
that "enough" is a thing,
a place, a state you can never
quite be.

I see you,
growing up in a home
that showed love
the best it knew how but
was still not filling
your whole heart. And

I see you,
seeking it elsewhere,
anywhere, with anyone who
wants to have their hands on you,
failing to love yourself
most of the time.

I see you,
trying to take on
a world you know
little about. You grew up,
after all, in a fairly homogeneous
family, town, community.
But you step out anyway,
scared, scarred, naive while
clinging to the familiar,
and in doing so, clinging
to a false self, but
at least she is familiar.
You have lost sight of
yourself.

I see you,
caught in
expectations, traditions,
opportunities
not pausing to consider
if they are what you want or
what is being handed to you.
But familiar is at least
less frightening than a larger
unknown.
You have lost sight of
yourself.

I see you,
sitting at the kitchen table
in tears, in pain,
wondering if this
is all there is and
pleading for it not to be,
desperate for more without
knowing what more exists or is.

I see you,
going through the motions
and getting it done while
draining your spirit, your soul
but showing up for others
yet not yourself.
You have lost sight of
yourself.

I see you,
the moment your world
pivots and grief tries to carry
you away with your grandmother
because you realize that life
is so short and you
have missed so much of it already.

I see you,
grasping for more while
the things you've tried
to build crumble and bring
more sadness and loss to try
and carry you away.

I see you,
letting her chisel away
from the inside, little by little,
racing against a world
trying to chisel away at you
from the outside.
Her voice is just a
whisper, the faintest memory,
but still a quiet reckoning.

I see you,
worn down by
hearing that you are
too feminist
too angry
too concerned about things,
people, situations beyond your reach,
too much, too loud
as you cry out for change
in the world around you.
And so
I see you
go quiet.

Until quiet almost breaks you.
Until quiet feels wrong.
Until quiet doesn't fix the pain, the
past.
Until her voice can
no longer be silenced within you.
Until you remember.
Until you see her.

Until you see yourself.

I see you,
discovering
reclaiming
blooming
stretching
shouting
remembering
reconnecting
forgiving
relearning.
I see you. I see me.
And I am beautiful.
I am still scared but
I am once again wild and free and
I am curious and demanding and
I am learning to define what
I need and write the terms of my story.
And finally,
I am enough and
I do not budge.

Raw

I haven't felt
anything this tender
in so long I thought
I'd forgotten how.
I'm no stranger
to big emotions -
anger
grief
regret
sadness
rage
resentment
bitterness.
It's just that
soft
and seen,
valued,
beautiful,
smart,
alive,
aren't things
I've known
in quite
some time.
They only feel
slightly stiff
as I try them back on,
but they still fit
and I love
the way I look
when wearing them.

Dancing with Fire

They were frightened
as they watched her grow.
A fire caught within her soul;
she grew more confident.
Passion and energy fueled her;
laughter erupted,
her smile could barely be contained.
She was discovering herself,
what she was capable of;
and the transformation was remarkable.
But would they be able to dance with fire?

Hungry

Show up on my doorstep,
hungry for me,
on the threshold of my mind,
arrive ready to devour
my thoughts.
Prepare to battle my anxieties alongside me,
and wage war with me
against the darkness there
when it creeps in like
a dense fog that smothers the light.
Wander slowly through
the fields of my musings,
wildflower thoughts
in brilliant colors
outpacing weeds that try to choke my mind
and pick for yourself
pretty things to remember me by
when we cannot be together.

Show up on my doorstep,
hungry for me.
At the entrance of my heart
move gently around my broken pieces.
If you dare, I'll even let you
hold them softly as we mend them.
Step boldly towards my love;
be warned against
taking it for granted,
but know its depth,
plunge into its comforting waves,
be held fully in the expanse of my adoration.

Show up on my doorstep,
hungry for me.
On the brink of my body,
tune yours to my composition;
the songs of my smile, my walk,
the lines of my curves
and the sweet hum
that rises from my lips
when you are near.

Consume the lyrics
written by my touch
on your skin;
swallow shyness as you
cover me with ravenous hands,
and feast until sated.

Show up on my doorstep,
hungry for me.
Before the gateway to my soul,
reverently pause,
take note of the wildness,
the passion,
dancing there like fire
awaiting someone brave enough
to fan the flames
and hold my hand,
pulling me close so that
our dreams can fuel each others'.

Show up on my doorstep,
hungry for me.
I am starving for you.

Tatoo drawing by: Galen Holland, Artist

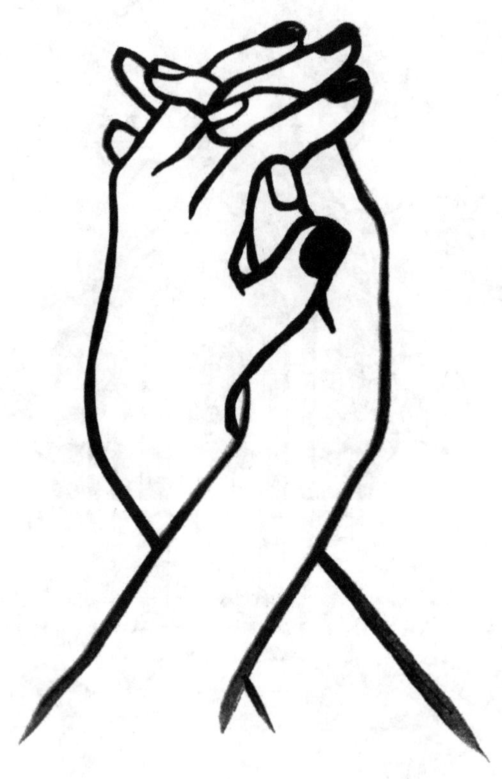

Acknowledgments

To everyone who has read any of my poetry in any of its draft or final forms, especially to those who encouraged me to think my words were worth sharing in print and at poetry open mic events, thank you. I dare not try to name you all because I will undoubtedly and unintentionally forget someone. Know that you are cherished and I am endlessly grateful.

About the Author

Angela (she/they) is a poet, an educator, and an idealist, currently living in the western part of North Carolina. This is her first published collection of poetry. Nearly a decade ago she had an earlier version of Dancing With Fire published in the NC Young Authors publication, wining in the Forever Young age category.

Angela has a PhD and a master's degree, both with a focus in counseling, and is a member of Mensa. With over two decades of a professional career in high school and college teaching and experience in mental health, she has received several awards and honors, including numerous recognitions as the former owner of an independent bookstore. Her favorite of these was the 1-star Google review the bookstore received for being "the wokest bookstore east of the Mississippi" which she turned into merchandise to raise money for The Trevor Project.

She is the mother of two inspiring daughters, one enthusiastic dog, and a host of plant babies that keep her on her toes.

Instagram: @thattattooedprofessor
website: angelawrites.studio

www.ingramcontent.com/pod-product-compliance
Lightning Source LLC
LaVergne TN
LVHW012331100826
845148LV00017B/2113

* 9 7 9 8 8 9 9 3 3 0 2 4 7 *